Laing

The Scarecrow Mystery

The Bobbsey Twins®

THE SCARECROW MYSTERY

Laura Lee Hope

Illustrated by John Speirs

WANDERER BOOKS

Published by
Simon & Schuster, Inc., New York

Copyright © 1984 by Stratemeyer Syndicate
All rights reserved
including the right of reproduction
in whole or in part in any form
Published by WANDERER BOOKS
A Division of Simon & Schuster, Inc.
Simon & Schuster Building
1230 Avenue of the Americas
New York, New York 10020

Manufactured in the United States of America
10 9 8 7 6 5 4 3 2 1

WANDERER and colophon are registered trademarks
of Simon & Schuster, Inc.

Library of Congress Cataloging in Publication Data

Hope, Laura Lee.
The scarecrow mystery.

(The Bobbsey twins ; 11)
Summary: A scarecrow who disappears and reappears at
other locations and an odd-shaped key lead the Bobbsey
twins into another mystery.
1. Children's stories, American. [1. Mystery and
detective stories] I. Speirs, John, ill. II. Title.
III. Series: Hope, Laura Lee. Bobbsey twins (1980–
; 11.
PZ7.H772Sc   1984   [Fic]   84-10414
ISBN 0-671-53238-3

Contents

·1·

A Strange Key

"I didn't know scarecrows could walk," said Freddie Bobbsey, peering out the window of the family station wagon.

"They can't," said his older brother Bert. "Whatever gave you that idea?"

" 'Cause there's one that did!" Freddie pointed to a scarecrow in a farmer's cornfield.

The Bobbseys were driving home to Lakeport after a day at the beach. Outside, the long summer twilight had deepened into darkness.

All four twins stared at the scarecrow standing silently in the moonlight as their car whizzed past. The funny-looking figure had a tall cowboy hat, a red bandanna around its neck, a plaid shirt and striped pants.

"What made you think that the scarecrow walked, Freddie?" asked dark-haired Nan Bobbsey. She and Bert were twelve years old, while their blond, curly-haired brother and sister were only six.

"He was scaring crows away from a different field this morning," Freddie replied. "Now he's walked all the way to that farm we just passed. I guess he wanted to help save someone else's corn, too."

Nan smiled and tousled the little boy's golden locks. "You must be mistaken, Freddie."

"No, I'm not!" he insisted.

"How do you know this one was the

same scarecrow you saw before?" his twin, Flossie, asked.

"I've got eyes, haven't I?"

And, indeed, Freddie did—big blue ones that usually sparkled with mischief. Just now his eyelids were drooping drowsily after the long day of sun and fun at the Bobbseys' favorite swimming resort.

"You saw that cowboy hat he had on, and his red neckerchief, didn't you?" Freddie went on.

"So what? That doesn't prove—" Bert stopped speaking as Mrs. Bobbsey turned from the front seat.

"Now don't start an argument," she said gently. "And, Freddie dear, don't you get cranky just because you're feeling sleepy."

The little boy folded his arms and thrust out his lower lip. "I know what I saw," he muttered stubbornly.

A few minutes later, as they got nearer

to Lakeport, Freddie pointed out the, window again. "That's where the scarecrow was this morning," he blurted. "Right by that windmill!"

A sign on the white fence around the cornfield said GREENBANK FARM.

This time, after a warning glance from their mother, none of the other twins argued with Freddie.

Next morning at breakfast, however, Flossie asked him, "Did that scarecrow really truly go to a different farm yesterday?"

Her little brother nodded his head up and down while he scooped big spoonfuls of cereal and milk into his mouth "Yes, he did! Honest, cross my heart!"

Bert chuckled good-naturedly. "Aw, Freddie, you were half asleep last night! Are you sure you didn't just *dream* you saw him in two different places?"

"No sirreeee! When we were going to the beach, he was at that farm with the windmill. And you know where we saw him on the way back!"

Bert sighed and rolled his eyes at Nan across the table. But his sister was too kind-hearted to lose patience with anyone, even Freddie at his stubbornest. "Arguing won't change anyone's mind," she pointed out softly.

"Well, I know what will," said Bert. "Charlie Mason asked me to go biking with him this morning. He wants to try out his new ten-speed bicycle. We'll ride out to Greenbank Farm, and I'll *ask* the farmer who lives there if he ever had a scarecrow in his cornfield!"

Just as the children were finishing breakfast, the telephone rang. Dinah Johnson, the black lady who helped Mrs. Bobbsey with the cooking and house-keeping, answered it in the kitchen.

"For you, Bert." Her jolly face appeared in the doorway. "Sounds like your pal Charlie."

Bert went off to talk to him. He came back looking disappointed.

"What's wrong?" Nan asked.

"Charlie can't go. He has to help his

Dad clean out their garage."

Nan nibbled her last piece of toast with marmalade. "Would you like company?"

Her twin brightened. "You bet! Want to come?"

"Sure, I could use some exercise!"

She and Bert were soon ready to start out on their bicycles. "Be careful now," their mother warned anxiously, "and watch out for cars! I'd rather you kept off the main roads."

"Don't worry, Mom," Bert promised. "We'll stay on the walking path along the shoulder."

With a wave of their hands, the two older twins pedaled off. Leaving Lakeport behind, they headed out into the sunny countryside.

It was a lovely summer morning. Bert and Nan enjoyed filling their lungs with fresh air as they biked along. Luckily, there was almost no traffic on the road, so they could hear birds singing and twittering in the trees, and now and then the mooing of cows.

Presently they saw a windmill ahead. Its vanes were turning lazily against the sky.

"Look! We're coming to Greenbank Farm!" Bert called out to Nan. "Now we'll soon be able to prove Freddie was seeing things!"

But they were in for a surprise. Today there was a scarecrow standing in the farmer's cornfield—a scarecrow with a cowboy hat and a red bandanna around its neck!

Odder yet, it was dressed in a plaid shirt and striped pants—*just like the scarecrow Freddie had pointed out last night in a different field!*

Bert and Nan slowed their bikes and stared with wide eyes. "I don't believe this," Bert mumbled.

"But it's there," said Nan.

"It wasn't last night."

"I know."

"Then how did it get here this morning?"

"Don't ask me."

They looked blankly at each other, and Bert scratched his head. The two twelve-year-olds didn't know what to make of such a strange mixup.

"Is this the right farm?" Bert asked.

Nan nodded. "There's the sign."

It said GREENBANK FARM, just as it had last night when there was no figure in the field.

"Well, there's one way to find out if we're both crazy," said Bert.

"How?"

"Keep going till we get to that other farm and see if it has a scarecrow, too."

Nan giggled. "Okay, but are you sure we can tell the right farm?"

"That's no problem. I remember it had a vegetable stand out front and a windbreak of pine trees."

The twins pedaled on. A couple of miles farther they came to the farm they were looking for. And once again they were startled.

This morning there was *no scarecrow* in sight!

Bert gulped. "This gets nuttier and nuttier!"

Nan burst out laughing at the expression on his face. "Never mind," she said. "Now we have a mystery to solve!"

In spite of their young age, the Bobbsey twins were good detectives and already had solved many baffling cases. Bert perked up at the chance of tackling a new mystery.

Leaning their bikes against the fence, the two walked into the cornfield. They were careful to tread between the rows of growing plants. "I'm sure it was right about here," said Bert.

Nan agreed. But even after searching around, they could find no hole where a post might have been placed to hold a scarecrow upright.

"Look!" Nan exclaimed suddenly. She bent down and picked something up.

"What did you find?" Bert asked.

She showed him a curious, old-fashioned-looking key. It had a fancy, curlicued handle and was made of yellowish metal.

"Bronze, I think," said Bert. "And it can't have been lying out here long, or it would have turned all greenish."

"And what's this?" Nan puzzled. She pointed to an odd symbol stamped on the handle: ♌

Neither twin had any idea what it might mean.

As they were about to leave, they saw the farmer drive up on his tractor. He had been tilling another field. Climbing down from the driver's seat, he took off his straw hat and mopped his forehead before going into the farmhouse. The twins waved, and he waved back with a friendly smile.

"Do you have a scarecrow?" Bert asked.

"Not any more, sonny. Used to, but some youngsters carried him off last Halloween, and I just never got around to making another."

"We thought we saw one here last night," said Nan.

The farmer chuckled. "Not unless the old one found some new clothes and stuffed himself with straw again. If he did, I sure haven't seen hide nor hair of him this morning. Maybe it was just some tramp or hitchhiker you saw."

Nan smiled and thanked him. As she and Bert were getting on their bikes, they saw a man with curly red hair strolling along the road toward them. He was staring at them keenly. But when he realized the two had noticed him, he smiled and nodded pleasantly. The twins pedaled off.

A few minutes later, a car passed them on their way back to Lakeport. The twins were surprised when they saw who was at the wheel. The driver was the man with curly red hair.

After a while, they sighted the windmill, which meant they were nearing Greenbank Farm. Then they saw a parked car. It was a snub-nosed yellow sedan, like the car that had passed them. It was pulled off the road, among some trees.

Ahead, they could see the curly-haired driver. He had gotten out and was walking toward the farm's cornfield. Again he smiled and nodded as the twins biked past.

Nan slowed down a moment or two later and glanced back over her shoulder. The man seemed to be going straight toward the scarecrow.

"Do you think we should go back and talk to him?" Nan called out to her brother. Bert shrugged and kept on. He seemed not to want to talk.

Nan was glad when they reached home. She was dying for a drink of cold water. Freddie ran to meet them. "What did you find out?" he yelled.

"You were right," said Nan. "The scarecrow was back where you saw it first."

Freddie let out a whoop and followed them into the house. He was eager to tell his little sister, who was playing with her dolls. "See, I was right!" he exclaimed.

Flossie's eyes grew big. "Maybe that scarecrow comes alive at night!"

Nan smiled, but Bert paid no attention to the small twins. He rushed to get a pencil and paper. "What are you writing down?" she asked.

"The license number of that car we saw!"

·2·

The Stolen Painting

"Smart idea!" said Nan. She knew now why Bert hadn't spoken when they biked past Greenbank Farm. Talking might have made him forget the license number. "Do you think that man may have something to do with the scarecrow mystery?"

"I don't know," Bert shrugged, "but I'd sure like to find out what he was up to! I'm going to see if a policeman can trace the number."

Nan went in the kitchen to get a drink. Dinah Johnson let the tap run a while to make sure the water was cool and bubbly. She also popped some ice cubes into the glass.

"Mmm, was that ever good!" said Nan after taking a long swallow. "Thank you, Dinah. I was *so-o-o* thirsty!"

"My goodness, child, you and Bert have been out riding your bicycles for a long while! It's almost time for lunch."

Nan's brown eyes twinkled. "That suits me! I'm already hungry again."

"Well, don't go 'way, hear? I'll soon have some food on the table!"

The dark-haired Bobbsey girl was good at drawing, so she was taking a summer art class at the Lakeport Museum. After lunch, she freshened up while Mrs. Bobbsey got ready to drive her to the museum in the family station wagon.

Meanwhile, Bert went off to find a policeman. The cop on the beat was a ruddy-faced officer named Hogan. He took out his notebook and copied down the license number Bert told him.

"Sounds like you Bobbseys are onto another mystery."

"Well, something strange happened last night," said Bert, "and we'd like to find out why. If we knew whose license number that was, it might help."

"Okay, I'll see what we can do." Officer Hogan unhooked the walkie-talkie from his belt and called the number in to Police Headquarters.

Bert thanked him and walked off to a locksmith's shop down the street. Inside, a balding man with glasses was working at a lathe.

Bert showed him the odd-looking bronze key. "Ever seen one like this before, Mr. Colby?"

"Hmm. No, not exactly . . . but I'm pretty sure I can tell you who made it."

"Gee, great!" Bert said eagerly. "Who did?"

"A locksmith named Ives over in Elm City. He used to make fancy keys like this to order, for folks who liked special hardware for their new houses. I'd recognize his work anywhere."

"Does he still make them?"

"No, the old man retired a while back, Bert. His son runs the business now. Maybe he could tell you where that key came from, if that's what you want to know."

"It is. Thanks a lot, Mr. Colby!"

At the same time Bert was leaving the locksmith's shop, Nan's art class was settling down to work. Desks and chairs had been provided in the big airy front room of the museum. Its walls were hung with paintings, and there were statues and other art objects on display.

The teacher, Mr. Oland, was one of the museum curators. "How many of you have heard about the robbery last night?" he asked.

Several hands went up.

"Well, if your family turned on the television news this morning or at lunchtime, you probably know all about it."

Mr. Oland told the class that a valuable painting had been stolen from the country home of a wealthy art-lover named Mr. Twiggin. According to the news reports, he had just added the picture to his collection and was holding a house party to show it to some friends.

"Before the party," the art teacher went on, "it seems Mr. Twiggin had a phone call from a famous thief known as *Le Fantome*. In French, that means 'The Phantom.' He is said to be one of the slickest art and jewel thieves in Europe. Anyhow, when he telephoned, he threatened to steal the new painting. So Mr. Twiggin hired special guards, and police cars were patrolling the roads all around his mansion. But in spite of that, the robber got in through an upper-story window and made off with the painting!"

By now, the children were listening eagerly.

"Here's what the stolen painting looks like," said Mr. Oland. He held up a clipping in full color from a Sunday newspaper and asked the young artists to pass it around. "Look at it carefully. See what *you* think of this painting. It's certainly causing a lot of excitement in the news! Then, for today's subject, I suggest you paint a picture of whatever this brings to mind."

Nan was eager for a closer look at the stolen masterpiece. It showed a French chateau on a hillside—a white castle-like building with a tall witch-hat tower. In the foreground was a farm field and a scarecrow.

I know what I'm going to paint a picture of! Nan decided. And she set to work at once with her watercolors to paint a picture of the cowboy-hatted scarecrow at Greenbank Farm.

Mr. Oland's remark about the excitement in the news was soon borne out. A television camera crew arrived at the museum. They had come to see what the art curators had to say about the stolen painting.

After talking to Mr. Oland, the interviewer decided to videotape the art class at work. His eye soon fell on Nan Bobbsey.

"Well, well, well!" he exclaimed, holding out the microphone toward her. "Aren't you one of those famous Bobbsey twins who solve so many mysteries?"

Nan felt embarrassed and a little nervous, so she merely smiled and nodded her head.

"And what do you make of last night's robbery, my dear?" the TV man asked.

Nan shrugged. "I . . . I really don't know anything about art thieves or how they work," she replied politely.

"But you certainly know something about crooks and mysterious crimes," he persisted.

"Well . . ." Nan hesitated, afraid of sounding silly or like a know-it-all. Then

she took a deep breath and said, "Well, I'll admit there are two things that especially puzzle me about the robbery."

"And what are those, Miss Bobbsey?"

"For one thing, why was the robber so eager to steal that particular painting? I imagine there must be others in Mr. Twiggin's art collection that are just as valuable."

The interviewer nodded thoughtfully. "Good question. And what's the other thing?"

"Well," said Nan, "I just can't see why a smart thief like *Le Fantome* would call beforehand and say he was going to steal the picture. Unless he's pretty dumb, he must have guessed the owner would get extra police protection—and that would make it all the harder to steal the picture!"

The TV man looked impressed. "I'd say you're a pretty smart young lady, Miss Bobbsey!"

Then he turned to face the camera. "In light of what Nan Bobbsey has just said,

I'm beginning to think last night's robbery may be not just a sensational crime, but an even more baffling mystery than the police realize. And in my humble opinion," he went on, "they might do worse than call in the Bobbsey twins to help them solve it!"

·3·

Lion Scare

The little twins were in the station wagon when Mrs. Bobbsey came to pick Nan up after class. She told them about her TV interview.

Flossie clapped her hands. "Then will we be able to see you on tele-ma-vision?"

"Maybe . . . if there's time enough on the newscast."

"How come they call that robber the Phantom?" said Freddie, who was blowing bubble gum. "Does he carry a fan in case he gets hot?"

Nan giggled. "Oh, Freddie, of course

not—don't be silly! A phantom is like a ghost. You know, sort of spooky and hard to see. I suppose they call him that because he sneaks around in the dark and nobody knows he's there."

"Is he invibzul?" her sister spoke up again.

"No, honey, he's not invisible," said Nan, trying not to laugh at the way Flossie mispronounced big words. "But I guess he's not very easy to catch, either."

The two girls stopped talking suddenly to stare at Freddie. The little boy was waving his hands and pointing proudly at a huge bubble he was blowing.

"Oh, Freddie! Don't blow it any bigger!" Flossie cried anxiously. She put both hands to her chubby little cheeks and squealed, *"Please!"*

A mischievous look came over her twin's face. Instead of stopping, he boastfully stuck his thumbs under his arms, fluttered his fingers, and kept right on blowing.

At the next moment the bubble popped! Its rubbery pieces spattered all over Freddie's nose and cheeks and chin. Some even got on his eyelids.

"See there now!" Nan chided him. "What did Flossie tell you?"

Freddie looked so surprised that at first Nan feared he might cry. She hastily set about scrubbing off the goo with a handkerchief. The little boy soon burst out laughing in relief, and so did his twin sister.

"Freddie's *face* was almost invibzul!" declared Flossie.

Soon after the station wagon pulled into the Bobbseys' drive, Bert came home. He had gone from the locksmith's shop to his father's lumberyard. He listened eagerly to what had happened at the museum. Then he told Nan about the key.

"Mr. Colby thinks it was made by an old locksmith named Ives in Elm City, so let's go see what we can find out. Sam Johnson has to deliver a load of lumber in

Elm City. He says we can ride over with him."

"Good!" said Nan. "Do you know the address?"

"Yes, I looked it up in the phone book. The shop's on Perry Street. Sam says that's just off Central Avenue."

Sam Johnson, who worked for Mr. Bobbsey at the lumberyard, was Dinah's husband. The couple lived on the top floor of the Bobbsey's house and were considered part of the family.

Bert kept watch out the window. Presently a blue pickup truck stopped in front of the house, and the big man at the wheel waved. "Here's Sam now," Bert exclaimed. "Let's go!"

Freddie and Flossie ran after the older twins.

"We want to go, too!" chanted Freddie.

"Yes, please take us!" Flossie chimed in.

It was hard to resist the expression on the little twins' faces. "I'm sorry," Nan said regretfully. "I wish we could take you two, but there's no room."

"Why not?" Flossie pleaded. "I could sit on your lap and Freddie could sit on Bert's."

"That's right! Hooray!" Freddie whooped. "Now you've *got* to take us!"

"No, we don't. That would make five in the front seat," said Nan, "and Daddy told us once that's against the law. Isn't that so, Sam?"

"Well . . . yes . . ." The burly black man, who seemed to take up half the space in the truck cab all by himself, wavered unhappily as his two little favorites threw him begging looks. "Tell you what, though, sugar—maybe we could all squeeze in, if your momma says it's all right and Bert doesn't mind riding in back with the wood."

"Gosh, no! That'll be fun!" Bert grinned and started to climb aboard over the load.

"But you stay sitting down all the way,

now mind, with your back up close to the cab—and hang on tight, or it's no deal!" Mr. Johnson got out to make sure Bert was safely seated and that there was no danger of the lumber shifting so as to hurt him while they were on the road. Then he took his place again behind the wheel, with Freddie crowded in between him and Nan, who was seated by the window with Flossie on her lap.

The blue pickup truck rumbled into motion as the twins called out good-bye to their mother and Dinah. The ladies waved back from the porch.

When they reached Elm City, Sam stopped in front of the locksmith shop on Perry Street, while the twins climbed down from the truck. Sam promised to return in ten or fifteen minutes.

A middle-aged man with thinning sandy hair came to the counter as Bert and Nan entered the shop. "Can I help you?"

"We hope so," Nan said. "Are you Mr. Ives?"

"That' right. Why?" the man asked curiously.

Bert showed him the bronze key. "Mr. Colby in Lakeport says this looks like your father's work. Can you tell us if he made it, please?"

A strange expression flickered over the locksmith's face. Nan thought he looked a bit startled. "Why, uh—yes, that does look sort of like the keys my dad used to make," George Ives replied. "Where did you get it?"

"We found it," Nan said politely but briefly. "Do you know the person he made it for?"

Ives frowned and shrugged. "That'd be pretty hard to say after all these years."

"But it's a very unusual key," said Bert. "Don't you keep any records?"

"Well, now, my dad might know—but he's retired, so he doesn't come to work in the shop any more. Look here, why don't you leave the key with me? I'll show it to him and see what he says."

The twins looked at each other uncomfortably.

"We'd rather not, Mr. Ives, if you don't mind," Nan said after a moment. "But I'll make you a drawing of it. That ought to be just as easy for your father to recognize."

Borrowing pencil and paper, she first traced the key's outline. Then she deftly filled in the curlicue design of the handle, and the odd squiggly symbol. Even the locksmith had to admit it looked fine. "Better leave your name and phone number so I can call you," he added.

The little twins had stayed outside. As Bert and Nan left the shop, Flossie came running up. She was alone, and her face looked flushed and excited. "We just saw a lion!" she cried.

"A *lion*?" her big brother and sister echoed in astonishment, and Bert said, "Where?"

"Around the corner! Come on, I'll show you! Freddie's keeping watch on it!" She tugged their arms and as the older twins ran along with her, Flossie asked, "Should we call the police?"

"I don't know," said Nan. "Wait'll we see what this is all about."

They were running in the opposite direction from Central Avenue. The next street was lined with factories and warehouses. Freddie was hiding behind some bushes in a vacant lot on the corner. "Over there!" he pointed. "Look!"

On the lawn in front of a building across the street stood a huge tawny lion. It looked ferocious and every few moments it lashed its tail and roared! The small twins shivered and covered their ears at the angry noise. But Bert only broke into chuckles.

Nan hugged her little brother and sister. "You needn't be afraid of that," she smiled. "It's just a"—she was about to say toy, but realized that wasn't the right word—"well, sort of like a statue."

"But it's alive!" Freddie insisted.

"No, it isn't," said Bert. "It's just got

machinery inside that makes it move its head and tail, and roar. You see, the company in that building is the Lion Manufacturing Company."

Flossie's eyes bugged. "Do they make *lions*?"

"Well, they made this one, I guess," Bert grinned, "but not real ones. The lion is just their company name and trademark. I think what they mostly make is factory machinery . . . you know, like those work robots you see pictures of in auto plants, that help put cars together as they move along the production line."

Nan added, "That mechanical lion just got put up about a year ago, if I remember rightly. It was shown in the news and on television because so many people drove by to see it."

Mr. Bobbsey, too, chuckled when he came home from the lumberyard that evening and heard about the lion adventure. "So my brave little fireman doesn't even run away from roaring lions!" he said, swinging Freddie up in the air.

Freddie loved to play with toy fire engines. Just now he couldn't help grinning down at his father from the sheer fun of being up so high. Even so, his grin was a bit shamefaced. "It wasn't a *real* lion, Daddy!"

"Never mind! The important thing is, you didn't get scared and run away. Maybe you'll grow up to be a big-game hunter!"

"My turn, my turn!" Flossie clamored.

"Okay," said Mr. Bobbsey, setting down Freddie. "Up you go, my little princess!"

Her golden curls fluttered about her head as he bounced her high in the air. Flossie squealed in delight. "What's a big-game hunter, Daddy?"

"Well, it's somebody who hunts big animals—like lions or tigers or rhinoceroses."

"Oh, no-o-o!" Flossie protested. "I

don't want Freddie to shoot *any* animals—even big, scary ones!"

Her tall, broad-shouldered father squeezed her tight and kissed her. "Come to think of it, sweetie, neither do I!"

Mr. Bobbsey was also interested to hear about Nan's TV interview and the scarecrow mystery. Nan showed him the bronze key. "Did you ever see one like this before, Daddy?"

It was just a chance question, on the spur of the moment, but to her surprise, he answered, "As a matter of fact, I have, Nan dear. I think that it must have been made by old Mr. Ives in Elm City."

Richard Bobbsey told his children that he had known Jason Ives before the elderly locksmith retired and turned his shop over to his son. "Sometimes Mr. Ives would make special keys and locks for houses that were built with lumber from our yard," Mr. Bobbsey explained. "We both belonged to the Lakeshore Builders

Society, and I went to a dinner in his honor when he retired."

After dinner, the family gathered in the living room to watch the evening news. "It's coming on right now!" Bert announced as he tuned the TV.

Everyone hoped Nan's interview would be shown. Tonight the program started out differently.

"I've just been handed a special bulletin!" said the newscaster. "Police are asking everyone who lives in or near Lakeport to be on the lookout for a notorious art thief called *Le Fantome,* or the Phantom. The car he may have used to carry out last night's daring robbery has just been found near the Lakeport waterfront!"

·4·

Airport Clue

"Wow! Maybe the Phantom's hiding out right here in town!" Bert gasped.

"Shhh!" said Mrs. Bobbsey. "Let's hear how they found his car."

The newscaster said that yesterday afternoon an unknown person had phoned the Elm City police, warning them that the famous thief had come to town to commit some new crime.

The caller said he had placed a snapshot of the crook under the windshield wiper of a parked police car. The photo was quickly checked by the FBI and the world police organization known as Interpol. Both said it was, indeed, *Le Fantome*.

"That, plus the telephone threat received by Mr. Twiggin, caused police to keep watch on the roads around his mansion yesterday evening," the newscaster went on. "The snapshot was also published in the paper. A woman at Elm City Airport saw it and recognized him as a man who had rented a car from her. She said he gave a false name and posed as an ordinary French tourist. After the police broadcast her description of the car it was seen by a Lakeport meter maid."

The thief's picture now appeared on the TV screen. He was a handsome, youngish-looking man with straight dark hair and rather sharp, hawklike features.

"His chin's got a dimple," said Freddie.

"That's called a cleft chin," said his mother. "I remember a movie star who had a chin like his."

"The hunted man's real name is Jac-

ques Dupré," the newscaster continued. "French police say he started out as a street orphan, and later worked as an artist's model and circus acrobat. Eventually he became one of the slickest jewel and art thieves in Europe, and was known in the underworld as the Phantom or the Stone Man.

"The law finally caught up with him, however, and he was sent to prison. He served five years behind bars before being let out, with time off for saving many lives by his brave rescue work during a prison fire. Since then, *Le Fantome* has apparently been lying low—until now!"

Next, the news program showed a reporter interviewing the art curator, Mr. Oland, at the Lakeport Museum about the stolen picture.

"The artist who painted it is a young woman named Liane Renard," Mr. Oland replied to the TV man's question. "She's

half French and half American. Many
critics consider her one of the most
talented artists in Europe."

Mademoiselle Renard's photo now
flashed on the screen. She was slender
and attractive, with ringleted reddish hair
down to her shoulders.

"Ooh, isn't she pretty!" exclaimed Flossie.

"Miss Renard just came over to America recently for a show of her work at a
New York art gallery," Mr. Oland said as
the interview continued. "One of her
paintings was sold to Mr. Twiggin even
before the show opened. Judging by
photographs, I would say it's her finest
work so far."

The news about the robbery ended
with a picture of the museum art class.
The children were shown painting pic-
tures inspired by the stolen masterpiece.
Then the camera moved in closer on Nan
Bobbsey painting with her watercolors.

"Uh-oh! Here comes the most interesting part of the whole newscast!" Bert said jokingly.

Nan blushed. But everyone in the family was proud of the way she talked with the interviewer. Her two questions about the robbery sounded just like the sort of things a smart detective might ask—namely, why did the thief want to steal that particular picture, and why would he be foolish enough to warn Mr. Twiggin beforehand?

Mr. Bobbsey laid aside his newspaper and got up from his easy chair to congratulate her. "Good work, my dear!" he said, giving Nan a hug and kiss. "I'm beginning to think you could be the first famous lady private eye, if you ever do decide to become a real detective!"

Later, when the news program went off the air and the Bobbseys were still chatting about the broadcast, the telephone rang. Nan went to the front hall to answer it.

"Are you the young lady who found a very unusual key in a farmer's field this morning?" a man's voice asked.

Nan was startled. "Why, uh . . . yes, I am," she replied.

"How lucky! I lost that key and was worried that I might not ever get it back," said the caller. "You deserve a reward, Miss Bobbsey. May I come to your house and get the key?"

"Well . . . yes, of course," said Nan. "That is, if you can tell me exactly what it looks like and can prove you own it."

"Don't worry, my dear, I can certainly do so. I shall visit you shortly."

Nan heard a click at the other end of the line. She put down the receiver, feeling slightly dazed—it had all happened so quickly and unexpectedly! Going back in the living room, she told her parents and Bert about the call.

"Didn't the man even ask where we live?" Mrs. Bobbsey inquired.

Nan shook her head, and Bert put in,

"Maybe he heard her name on the news show and looked us up in the phone book. I'd say the big question is how did he know she found that key."

"That's what I'd like to know, too," said Nan. "Another funny thing is that he spoke with a French accent!"

Just then a loud barking was heard from outside. It sounded like Waggo. The Bobbseys' little fox terrier had gone out to play with Freddie and Flossie in the backyard. The little twins themselves came running into the house moments later.

"A spooky scarecrow is chasing us!" cried Freddie.

·5·

Spooky Traces

Bert and Nan ran outside to see what had frightened the small twins. In the twilight, a weird looking scarecrow face peered at them over the back fence! Then it stuck its thumbs in its ears and waggled its fingers!

"I'll bet I know who that scarecrow is!" Bert dashed angrily toward the fence.

But the fake strawman was already running off down the alley. He paused just long enough to doff his hat and pull off the paper-bag mask he had used to disguise himself. Then he stuck out his tongue and jeered at the Bobbseys before taking to his heels again.

"It's Danny Rugg!" said Nan.

"You're telling me!" Bert steamed. "I'm going to fix that wise guy once and for all!"

Danny was in the same grade as the two older twins, but he was an unpleasant boy who enjoyed teasing children smaller than himself. He often played tricks on Freddie and Flossie, because more than once their big brother had used his fists to teach Danny a well-deserved lesson.

Bert didn't even bother to unlatch the back gate. He was about to vault over the fence and go after the little twins' tormenter, but Nan stopped him. "Don't waste your time on that dumb old bully. That's just what he wants—to get you all worked up and mad enough to chase him. It makes him feel important."

Bert nodded reluctantly. "Guess you're right. He probably has his bike all ready and waiting at the end of the alley. But I wonder what made him think of dressing up like a scarecrow?"

Freddie looked sheepish. He admitted he had been telling other children in the neighborhood about the "live scarecrow" they had seen the night before. "Danny must've heard me," he mumbled.

"Never mind, dear." Nan gave the little boy a hug. "I don't think he'll come back."

"If he does," Bert added, "I'll turn the hose on him!"

The older twins went back in the house. Mr. Bobbsey had retired to the den to do some paper work he had brought home from the lumberyard. Mrs. Bobbsey and Dinah were putting away the dinner things and making the kitchen tidy.

Bert flopped down on the sofa. "That guy who phoned about the key, Nan, how do you suppose he found out you had it?"

Nan was still puzzling over the same question. "If we knew that," she said, settling herself in an easy chair, "I have a feeling we might be a little closer to solving the scarecrow mystery."

"He couldn't have found out from the locksmith," Bert mused.

"No, because we never told Mr. Ives where we found it. But the caller knew I'd picked it up in a farmer's field."

Bert shot a startled glance at his sister. "Do you suppose he could be that curly-haired guy we saw this morning?"

"Maybe." Nan brooded for a moment with her chin in her hands. Then she sighed and shrugged. "I guess we'll just have to wait till he comes here to find out."

She got up from her chair, adding, "The key's in my purse. I'd better go get it. He may be here any minute!"

"Don't give him the key unless he can prove it's his," Bert advised.

Nan nodded emphatically. "I already told him on the phone that I wouldn't."

When she returned to the living room

with her purse, Bert also urged her not to show her caller the key unless he could describe it exactly. Nan said she had made this clear, too.

While they waited for the unknown caller to arrive, the twins watched a TV show, which soon bored them. Then they worked on a jigsaw puzzle. Freddie and Flossie looked on and helped to fit in a piece now and then. By bedtime, however—much to everyone's disappointment—the doorbell still had not rung.

"Looks like he's not coming," said Bert.

"Maybe he'll call tomorrow," Nan said, hoping.

Late that night, Bert awoke with a start. He had been having a strange dream about a scarecrow prowling around in the house. *Whew!* he thought, rolling over in the darkness. *That sure seemed real. I'm glad it was just a dream!*

Bert was unable to drift back to sleep. Finally he got out of bed quietly, so as not

to wake up Freddie, and put on his bathrobe. Then he started downstairs to get a glass of milk.

Br-r-r! It's chilly, Bert thought with a shiver. Uh, oh . . . no wonder!

Someone had left the window open at the foot of the stairs, despite a weather forecast of cold air rolling down from Canada.

Bert closed the window and went into the kitchen to get the milk out of the refrigerator. He poured himself a glassful and began to sip it.

Suddenly his eyebrows rose. He had just heard a faint noise from the living room. Or at least he *thought* he had heard something.

Bert listened carefully. *There it was again!* A chill trickled down his spine as he remembered his spooky dream about the scarecrow. He could feel his skin turning to gooseflesh.

But he was too brave to be scared by what might be just his imagination. Bert set his glass down softly on the table and tiptoed into the living room.

Everything seemed quiet. He switched on the light and looked around. The room was empty. Bert heaved a sigh of relief and went back in the kitchen to finish his milk.

Next morning at the breakfast table, he told the other twins about his dream and his scary little midnight adventure.

Nan's eyes widened anxiously. "Did you say the window was open when you came downstairs?"

Bert nodded in surprise. "Yes, why?"

Instead of answering, Nan got up and darted into the living room. She went straight to the little table under the wall mirror, where she had left her purse the night before.

Bert followed. "What's the matter?" he asked as she searched for her purse.

"My purse!" Nan turned and flashed her brother a look of dismay. "It's *gone!*"

Bert groaned and dashed to the window

he had closed last night. He opened it and examined the screen. "Oh, no-o-o!" he muttered, slapping his forehead.

"Someone got in that way?" Nan asked, even though she had already guessed the answer.

"See for yourself!"

The screen had been neatly cut all around the inner edge of the frame! The intruder would just have had to lift the mesh up out of his way in order to climb in!

Then Nan noticed something else . . . something Bert had been too busy checking the screen to notice. "Look!" she exclaimed, pointing toward the floor.

On the carpet, directly below the windowsill, lay several wisps of straw!

A Surprise Visitor

Freddie and Flossie came running into the living room to see what the older twins had found.

"Does that mean a *scarecrow* got in our house last night?" gasped Flossie, her blue eyes big and round.

"I guess that's what we're supposed to think," Bert said.

Freddie hopped up and down with an excited look on his chubby little face. "See? I told you scarecrows can walk!"

Bert chuckled ruefully and rumpled his

little brother's mop of blond hair. "I meant that's what whoever broke in *wants* us to think. I didn't say that's what I *did* think."

There was more good-natured chatter as the Bobbsey twins went back to the table to finish their breakfast. But the chatter soon dwindled to a mystified silence.

Bert and Nan looked at each other glumly across the table. Both were thinking the same thing: now that the bronze key had been stolen, they had lost their one real clue to the scarecrow mystery!

Mrs. Bobbsey thought the robbery should be reported. After breakfast she phoned the police, and a scout car soon pulled up outside. The two officers from the car examined the screen and one wrote down what had happened.

"I have a hunch the burglar was hiding in the living room when I came downstairs," Bert told them. "Then he ducked out the front door while I was in the kitchen. That could've been the noise I heard."

"Probably so," the policeman with the notebook said. "Well, this case will go to the burglary squad, and our men will do what they can. But I'm afraid it won't be easy to track down the thief with so little to go on."

Soon after the police car drove away, another car stopped in front of the Bobbseys' house. This one was big and shiny and expensive-looking. A well-dressed, middle-aged man got out and rang the doorbell. Dinah Johnson went to answer it.

"I'd like to see Bert and Nan Bobbsey," the man said and handed her his calling card.

The twins read the card in surprise. It said:

> *Hubert G. Caryll, Manager*
> *Lion Manufacturing Company*

They politely invited their visitor to sit down.

"I believe you two are the ones who recently found a key?" Mr. Caryll began. "Quite an unusual-looking one, made of bronze?"

Nan nodded, "Yes, sir," and waited for him to explain further.

"I believe it may be mine," he went on. "George Ives, who runs the locksmith shop in Elm City, told me about it. He showed me your drawing, and I recognized it right away. You see, that key has belonged to my family a long time, so there are sentimental memories attached to it."

Mr. Caryll smiled and took out his wallet.

"Need I add, you both deserve a reward for being so honest and going to so much trouble to find the owner."

"I'm sorry, Mr. Caryll," Nan said, "but the key was stolen last night."

The visitor's face fell. *"Stolen?"*

"Yes, sir," Bert said. "A burglar broke in through that window right over there."

"But why would he bother to steal a mere key?"

"It was in my purse," Nan explained.

"Oh, I see." Mr. Caryll nodded gloomily. "So he snatched that for whatever money was in it."

"We reported the robbery to the police," Bert added. "They were here just before you came."

"Well, then, there's nothing more to be done." Hubert G. Caryll sighed and stood up. "It's my own fault, I dare say, for not getting in touch with you more promptly. But George Ives just told me about the key last night. Where did you find it, by the way?"

"In a field, between Lakeport and Elm City," Nan replied.

"How odd! I wonder how it got there?" But Mr. Caryll did not seem much interested in his own question. "I trust you'll let me know, my dear, if the police recover your purse?"

"Yes, sir, I will," Nan promised.

After their visitor left, she turned to her twin with a wry little smile. "So where does that leave us on the scarecrow mystery?"

Bert snapped his fingers. "We still have one lead to follow up."

"What do you mean?"

"The license number of that car we saw yesterday morning."

"You're right! The one driven by that man who saw us coming out of the farmer's field!"

The two got their bicycles out of the garage and rode around the neighborhood looking for Officer Hogan. They found him on a street corner, keeping an eye on traffic.

"Did you ever trace that license number I gave you?" Bert asked him.

"You bet we did—in fact, you deserve a pat on the back for that, Bert!"

"How come?"

"It turned out that that was the license number of the car the Phantom rented at the airport."

"The *Phantom!*" Bert stared in surprise. "You mean the thief who stole that painting?"

"Right! It was your report that led the state troopers and the FBI to concentrate their search on this area. And it sure paid off!" The big, ruddy-faced policeman put both hands on his hips and beamed at Bert.

"A yellow sedan?" Bert inquired.

"That's the one. I saw it myself after it was hauled in to the auto pound."

The twins looked at each other uncertainly. "But the picture of the Phantom that was shown on TV didn't look anything like the man we saw driving that car," Nan said in a puzzled voice.

"It didn't, eh? What did the fellow you saw look like, honey?"

"He had sort of a round face and red, curly hair. But if that picture of the thief was right, the Phantom has—well, sort of sharp features and straight dark hair."

"Hmm." Officer Hogan frowned thoughtfully and scratched his jaw. "Well, the man you saw may have been his accomplice. Or maybe the Phantom got scared and didn't want to risk turning the car back in at the airport once he realized the police were wise to him. So he might have sold it to some unsuspecting buyer."

"And when the curly-haired guy realized who it was he had bought it from," said Bert, "he got scared, too, and just walked off and left it parked on the street?"

"Something like that," said the policeman. "Anyhow, I'll radio his description to Headquarters. If the fellow can be traced, maybe he can help us track down the Phantom!" Unhooking the walkie-talkie from his belt, Officer Hogan reported what the twins had just told him.

Bert and Nan biked home thoughtfully.

"I'm pretty sure of one thing," Bert remarked as they parked their bicycles in the garage.

"What's that?"

"Somehow the scarecrow mystery is connected to that art robbery."

Nan nodded. "I think so, too—especially when I remember how that man sounded on the phone last night when he called about the key!"

You mean his accent?"

"Right. I'm sure it was French. And that gives me an idea, Bert!"

Her brother grinned. "Okay, I'll have to admit, your ideas are usually pretty good. Let's hear it."

"Remember, on the news, Mr. Oland said the artist who painted the stolen picture was half French? Liane Renard, I think her name was. Well, if we're right about the scarecrow mystery being connected to the art robbery, maybe *she'd* know something about the key!"

Bert frowned as they walked into the

house. "But what good does that do us? The art gallery that's showing her paintings is in New York."

Nan giggled boldly. "Okay, so she's there, and we're here. What are telephones for?"

First she asked her mother's permission to make a long-distance call to New York City. Then she phoned the museum to make sure of the painter's name and the name of the art gallery.

Bert stood by with keen interest as she dialed New York information to find out the gallery's number. Then she dialed again and asked to speak to the director of the gallery.

"Yes, may I help you?" a man's voice inquired politely.

Nan explained why she was calling and asked to speak to the woman painter.

"I'm sorry, that's impossible." The director sounded worried. "Mademoiselle Renard checked out of her hotel quite unexpectedly last night, and we haven't heard from her since!"

·7·

Star Sign

Bert saw the startled look on his sister's face as she thanked the gallery director and hung up the phone. "What's the matter?" he asked.

"Liane Renard has disappeared!"

"Jumpin' jellybeans! Then you were right, Nan—she must be mixed up in the mystery!"

"It looks that way. But we won't learn a thing if we can't talk to her."

Freddie and Flossie had gone outside to play. The big twins wandered into the kitchen in search of food to ease their eleven o'clock hunger pangs.

"Well, I suppose a peanut-butter cookie or two won't do any harm," Dinah Johnson allowed. "But mind you don't spoil your lunch!"

"We won't," Bert promised, heading straight for the cookie jar.

The housekeeper, enjoying a pause from kitchen chores, was reading the paper and sipping tea before beginning to prepare the midday meal. The twins heard her chuckle.

"What are you reading, Dinah?" Nan asked.

"That astrology column—*Your Future in the Stars!* I always like to read what's in store for people born under my sign. 'Course, it hardly ever comes true, but I keep reading anyhow!"

"What do you mean, 'born under your sign'?" Bert asked.

"Well, you know, when you look up at night, the stars aren't always in the same place in the sky 'cause the earth keeps whirling around. But these astrology folks claim that where the stars were when you were born is mighty important," Dinah explained. "They divide up the sky into twelve different parts. Each one has a sign named for the main bunch of stars in it. Now, mine is called Taurus. . . ."

Dinah took out a pencil and drew her sign on one edge of the newspaper—a circle with a half-circle on top of it. "You see, it's sort of like a bull's head with horns. That's 'cause folks long ago used to think the stars in that part looked like the outline of a bull—'least, that's how I understand it—and they're the stars that were just rising when I was born."

"Dinah, you're a wonder!" said Bert. "That's the first time anyone ever explained to me what that astrology stuff was all about."

The cook smiled fondly at him over the rim of her teacup. "'Course, that doesn't prove it's true, honey," she added, setting the cup down in its saucer. "Now, today it says here under the sign of Taurus that

I'm going to help someone in my family solve a problem."

An excited look had come over Nan's face. She snapped her fingers and gave the plump woman a hug. "Well, that astrology column's right, Dinah—'cause *we're* your family and *you* just did!"

"Did what, sweetie?"

"Helped me solve a problem!"

Bert looked on, mystified by his sister's outburst. "What's that supposed to mean?"

"Tell you later! First I have to look something up at the library. Want to come along?"

"Sure, why not?"

The twins were wheeling their bicycles out of the garage again when their mother called from an open window. "Where are you two going?"

"The library," Bert called back. "Why?"

"Don't be late for lunch! I want us to eat

early, so we can go downtown—that is, if
you two want to come along. I have some
shopping to do at the department store."

"You bet!" said Bert. "Count me in."

"Me too," said Nan. "We won't be long,
Mom!"

At the library, Nan looked up some
book numbers in the catalog. Then she
found the right bookshelf and began leaf-
ing through one of the volumes she had
looked up. Bert noticed that it was a book
on astrology.

Suddenly Nan brightened and whispered, "I've found it! Look here, Bert!"

She was pointing to a squiggly symbol
on the book page. At first Bert didn't understand what she meant. Then he caught
on. "Hey, that's the sign that was stamped
on the bronze key!"

"Right! The sign of *Leo the Lion!*"

Bert remembered something else.
"And that man who came for the key—Mr.
Caryll! He was the manager of—"

"—the Lion Manufacturing Company!" Nan chimed in.

"Then I guess that proves the key was his, all right," her twin reflected, lowering his voice again as he saw a librarian frown.

"Maybe so," Nan whispered. "I just wish we'd asked him what it was the key to!"

The table was set for lunch by the time they got home. Dinah was frying hamburgers. When the meal was over and Freddie's and Flossie's hands and faces had been washed, Mrs. Bobbsey got out the family station wagon and started downtown with all four twins.

"There's a white sale on," she remarked as they left the car in the store's parking garage, "so I want to see about some new sheets and pillowcases—and then I think all you twins can use some new jeans and shorts."

The summer sale ads in the local paper

had drawn many shoppers. As the Bobbseys made their way through the throngs of people alongside the counters on the first floor, Bert squeezed his sister's hand. "Nan, look!"

"Where?"

"Over there!" Bert pointed discreetly.

A man with curly red hair was edging past the shoppers in the next aisle. Nan gasped. He was the man they had seen near the farmer's fields—and perhaps also the man with the French accent who had phoned to inquire about the bronze key!

"Mom, Nan and I just saw someone we want to talk to!" Bert murmured hastily. "We'll meet you in the linen department!"

"All right, dear, but don't be long!"

The two older twins hurried in pursuit of the curly-haired man. But it was hard to go very fast when they had to travel through the crowd and dodge other shoppers.

Somehow they managed to keep the mystery man in sight. They saw him step aboard an elevator. Before they could reach it, the elevator door slid shut and the indicator arrow swung upward.

"Oh, we've lost him!" said Nan.

"Never mind! Maybe we can still catch him!" Bert tugged his sister toward the escalator.

To the eager twins, the stairs seemed to move at a snail's speed. And the people ahead prevented them from climbing the steps any faster.

When they reached the next floor, the elevator had already let out passengers and gone on upward. The same thing happened on 3. On the top floor, 4, they finally caught up with the elevator while its door was still open. But the curly-haired man was nowhere in sight!

"Just our luck!" Bert grumbled.

He and Nan kept their eyes peeled on the way back down, but failed to get a glimpse of the person they were looking for. When they finally rejoined their mother, she greeted them anxiously.

"Freddie and Flossie wandered off when I wasn't looking! Will you two try to find them?"

"Sure thing, Mom. We'll find them, don't worry!" Nan promised, giving her a quick hug.

"Thank you, dears!" Mrs. Bobbsey was still waiting for her order to be rung up. "I'll stay right here till you get back, so we won't all get separated."

The two older twins hurried off. Their goldenhaired little sister and brother were nowhere in sight. But presently they saw a familiar face, that of Danny Rugg. He was with one of his pals, Elmer Garvin.

"What's the matter with you nitwit Bobbseys? Can't you keep track of each other?" he jeered.

Seeing the angry light of suspicion that

flared in Bert's eyes, Danny tried to duck out of reach. But Bert was too quick and grabbed him by the arm. "Hold it! What makes you think we can't keep track of each other?"

The bully shrugged uncomfortably. "You were looking around for some-body—anyone could tell that. So I figured you must be hunting for those little punks."

Bert shook Danny. "Don't call my brother and sister names!"

"Why not? They go wandering around like little goofs and don't even know enough to stay with whoever brought 'em here!"

"You mean you've seen them?"

"I didn't say that!" Danny tried to push Bert away roughly, but the Bobbsey boy had seen the guilty look on Elmer Garvin's face. That look told him his suspicion was correct.

"You've seen them, all right!" Bert

doubled up his fist. "And I'll bet you teased them and scared them off—*that's* why they're lost!"

"You're crazy!" Danny's voice was sulky. He squirmed frantically in Bert's grasp and clenched his own fists, hoping a bold front might scare off the Bobbsey boy. But it didn't.

"I'll give you till I count ten," Bert warned. "Then you'd better tell the truth, or I'm going to punch you right in the nose, Danny Rugg!"

"All right, all right! We did see them, but we didn't touch 'em! We just made faces at 'em, that's all!"

Bert's lip curled scornfully. "You two aren't even worth wasting a good punch on!" He shoved Danny backward against Elmer Garvin. Both boys lost their balance and tumbled in a heap. "Come on, Nan—let's go!"

As the older twins walked away, Nan murmured to her brother, "I don't blame you for getting mad at Danny and that

Elmer Garvin—they probably did scare Freddie and Flossie. But fighting with Danny never does any good."

Bert shrugged impatiently. "Maybe not, but that wise guy gets me so sore I can't help it!"

"Try not to let him get under your skin."

"Okay, Sis—if you say so." Bert's good-natured grin suddenly changed to a look of relief. "Hey, there they are!" he pointed.

The little twins were in a cluster of on-lookers. Both were standing on tiptoe and craning for a better look at a spectacle in the front window. People outside the store were also staring in at the display.

A figure in a chef's hat and apron was posed over a barbecue stove. He looked as if he were grilling hamburgers at a cookout. But he was standing absolutely motionless!

"Hey, is that guy alive—or just a wax dummy?" Bert muttered.

"Search me," said Nan. "He looks like a real person, but . . . but if he's alive, how can he stand so still?"

The two moved closer for a better look. Then both twins gasped as they recognized the living statue. *He was the curly-haired man they had seen and chased when they first entered the store!*

·8·

Mister Falseface

The older twins stared in astonishment. Then a look of understanding flashed between them. "Are you thinking the same thing I am?" Nan whispered.

Her brother hissed back, "You bet! Something tells me we've just solved the scarecrow mystery!"

"That man in the window could've been the scarecrow we saw coming back from the beach!"

"Right! He just dressed up in the scarecrow's outfit for a disguise. And whenever he saw any car lights coming, he'd freeze motionless, like this guy in the window's doing now."

"The same as he did when we drove by that night," Nan added, "to make us think he really *was* a scarecrow."

Bert nodded emphatically. "And you know *why*, Nan?"

"He was trying not to be spotted by any police cars that were out patrolling the roads."

"Check! So he must be the thief who stole the pai—" Bert's voice trailed off uncertainly. He put one fist on his hip, scratched his head and frowned at his sister. "There's only one thing wrong with our theory, Nan."

"I know. That man in the window doesn't look anything like the thief's picture we saw on TV."

"Right! The Phantom had straight dark hair, didn't he?"

"Yes . . . but, of course, this man's curly red hair could just be a wig," Nan whispered.

"Hmm, could be," Bert agreed. "But their features were different, too. The Phantom was sort of hawk-faced, as I recall, and this man's face looks more roundish, at least from here."

Nan brooded silently and continued to stare at the statue-like figure. He seemed not to have moved a hair. Some of the spectators were mystified. Others seemed certain the figure was human, not a wax dummy. The twins, of course, knew he was alive, having seen him before.

"Maybe he has some way to disguise his features, too, Bert," Nan said finally.

"Maybe so. I'd sure like to see that photograph of the Phantom again," her brother said.

"We *might* be able to see it at the TV station," said Nan. "The studio's just in the next block."

"Hey, that's a great idea!" Bert exclaimed.

They wormed their way through the crowd to get Freddie and Flossie, and then took the smaller twins back to Mrs. Bobbsey. She was still waiting at the white sale counter.

Bert explained where he and Nan wanted to go. Their mother gave permission, and the two hurried out of the store and down the block.

Inside the studio, Nan asked the lady at the reception desk if they could speak to the reporter who had interviewed her at the museum. "I think one of the cameramen called him Vince."

"You certainly may, dear, if he's in. Just let me check." The young woman dialed a number and spoke on the phone, then hung up and smiled at Nan. "Take the elevator to the second floor. Vince will be waiting when you step off."

The reporter also greeted them with a smile. "So this is your brother, is he? And what can I do for you two Bobbseys?"

"Could we see that photograph of the Phantom that you showed on the news program?" said Nan.

"Sure, no problem." He led them into the newsroom and made a phone call. A picture of the famous thief, Jacques Dupré, soon appeared on a television monitor screen. He had straight dark hair and sharp features, as the twins had remembered, and also a cleft chin. The reporter was watching with keen interest. "Are you two detectives on another mystery trail?"

Bert grinned. "Well . . . sort of."

"If you're close to cracking this case, would you mind letting me know when you solve it?"

Nan giggled. "Okay, it's a deal! And thanks a lot for showing us the Phantom's picture."

As the twins walked back to the store, Bert said, "You know, I just thought of something, Nan. Remember the thief's other nickname?"

"Sure, the Stone Man."

Bert nodded. "I thought that was because he stole jewels and probably knew a lot about precious stones. But maybe the *real* reason is that he can stand as still as a stone statue!"

"I'll bet you're right!" Nan exclaimed. "And that would also fit in with what the newscaster said about him once working as an artist's model. He'd have to stand very still whenever he was posing for an artist!"

The twins were worried when they discovered that the "live wax dummy" was now gone from the store window. But a floorwalker assured them he had not left. "He's just taking a coffee break in the employees' lounge on the third floor."

The twins thanked him and started up the escalator. After looking around, they found a door marked EMPLOYEES ONLY. Nan glanced at her brother. "Think this is the lounge?"

Bert crossed his fingers. "Let's find out." He pushed open the door.

Inside, the man with curly red hair was seated on a green, vinyl-covered sofa, sipping coffee from a plastic foam cup. A startled look crossed his face as he saw the Bobbsey twins. He gulped down his coffee, tossed the cup in a wastebasket and rose to go out the door.

Bert stopped him. "Excuse me, but aren't you the man we saw at those two farms yesterday?"

The curly-haired man shook his head and tried to brush past. Bert reached up and rubbed the man's jaw. Soft makeup putty came off on his fingers! *Underneath, the man had a cleft chin!"*

"He's the Phantom!" Nan cried.

Bert tried to grab a handful of curly red hair, but the man seized his wrist gently. "Easy, my young friend—no need to pull off my wig. I'm Jacques Dupré, all right. You two have found me out." There was a rueful smile on his lips, and he spoke with a French accent.

"Your face looks rounder than it does in your photograph," said Nan. "How did you change it?"

"More makeup, *cherie*. Mostly it is because each cheek is stuffed with facial tissue."

The famous thief seemed so friendly that the twins were puzzled over what to do next. It almost seemed impolite to have him arrested.

"If you're *Le Fantome*, we'll have to call the police," Nan said almost apologetically.

"You must do whatever seems right, my dear. But I assure you I have been going straight ever since I got out of prison—and I did *not* steal that painting."

"Then why pose as a scarecrow?" said Bert. "You must've been trying to sneak up to Mr. Twiggin's mansion without being nabbed by the police."

Jacques Dupré nodded. "*Oui*, that is so. But I repeat, I did not steal the painting. I was merely going there to recover an important paper for a . . . for a certain friend of mine."

He would not explain why the paper

was important, however, or tell them who
his friend was.

The Bobbseys were inclined to believe
the mild-mannered Frenchman. Nan also
remembered that the phone call the
Phantom was said to have made, threaten-
ing to steal the painting, had never made
sense to her in the first place.

"If you'll just trust us and tell us the
whole story," she pleaded, "we'll do our
best to help you!"

Dupré was silent for a moment, con-
sidering. "You are very kind, *cherie*. Before I can accept your offer, however, I
must consult my friend. This means you
would have to trust *me* first."

He said he would be posing in the window until the store closed at 5:30. If his
friend agreed to Nan's offer, the two
would meet the Bobbseys in the park near
the store at six o'clock. "Otherwise, I shall
come alone and go with you to Police
Headquarters. Here, by the way, is the
bronze key I stole from your house."

The twins took it and looked at each other uneasily. Each drew a deep breath. "All right," Nan said to Dupré. "We'll trust you."

They watched him pose in the store window for the rest of the afternoon. As closing time neared, they hurried home for a quick bite of supper. Then they returned downtown and settled themselves on a park bench to wait.

Six o'clock chimed from the town hall clock. As the minutes passed, the twins' hearts sank. Perhaps the crook had tricked them! But suddenly they saw the Frenchman walking toward them. An attractive young woman was with him.

"She's the painter," Nan exclaimed, "Liane Renard!"

9

The Mysterious Letter

Mademoiselle Renard smiled at the twins. "So you are the clever young detectives who caught the famous Phantom!"

Nan and Bert smiled back and shook hands with the artist as Jacques Dupré introduced them.

"My sister tried to call you in New York this morning," said Bert. "She had a hunch you might know something about that bronze key."

"Well, she was right. I do know something about it, but not as much as I would *like* to know. Now that you Bobbseys have offered to help, perhaps we can solve the mystery together!"

Liane Renard spoke almost like an American. She explained that she had learned English from her American mother, who had married a poor country lawyer in France. Her mother's family had been very much against the marriage, and afterward would have nothing to do with her.

Liane related all this as she and the Bobbsey twins and Jacques Dupré strolled about the park.

"Did your mother ever come back to the United States?" Bert asked.

Liane shook her head sadly, saying both her parents had passed away. She herself had been raised in France, and after attending art school in Paris, had become a successful painter.

"Several months after my mother died," Liane went on, "a letter for her came from

America. It was from my grandfather. He did not know she had passed away. He wrote in the letter that he regretted very much having been so unkind to her, and that he longed to see her again, because all of his loved ones were now gone, except for her."

"Did you write back to him?" asked Nan.

"I couldn't. You see, there was no return address. My grandfather wrote that he had purposely not used his regular printed stationery for fear she might return his letter unopened if she knew who it was from."

"That sounds as though he had tried to write her before," Bert said, "and she wouldn't answer his letters."

"Exactly," said Liane. "Which only made me want to get in touch with him all the more. But unhappily I did not know where or how. All I had to go on was an Elm City postmark."

"Elm City?" the twins echoed in surprise.

"Yes." The attractive young artist nodded. "At that time, of course, I did not yet know that one of my paintings would be sold to someone who lived near Elm City. However, a New York art gallery was planning to exhibit some of my pictures, and I would be coming to America for the show, so I hoped to locate my grandfather then. But a few weeks later, another letter from him arrrived."

"Did it give his address?" Bert inquired.

"No, and this second letter upset me very much. It was written in a strange, hasty scrawl, as if my grandfather was frightened and had only moments to put down all he wanted to tell. He said he was ill and was being held prisoner, but that he would try to sneak out this brief message with the help of an electrical repairman."

"How strange!" said Nan.

"Yes, and most worrisome. His message ended: *Please come and help me as soon as possible!*"

"How could you come if you didn't know where to find him?" Bert put in.

"Naturally, I couldn't. But he assumed my mother would get the message—and he enclosed that bronze key. No doubt he expected her to recognize it, and thought the key would tell her exactly where he was being held. But to me it meant absolutely nothing."

Liane added that the repairman had countersigned his name at the bottom. Even now, her worries were not over. She related that soon after she got the strange message, her studio was broken into and ransacked.

"Who on earth would do that?" Nan asked.

"Presumably the same person who was holding my grandfather prisoner."

"But wasn't he in America?" Bert objected.

"True, but he could have paid French thugs to do the breaking in."

"What do you suppose they were after?"

Liane shrugged. "Most likely the message. Keys can be replaced, but that letter in my grandfather's writing would be proof that he was being held prisoner, if I took it to the American police, as I intended to do."

Nan gasped. "You mean it's gone?"

"Unfortunately, yes. You see, I had been carrying the letter in my handbag, but I feared the thugs might return and try again to steal it. So I hid the letter between the canvas and frame of one of my paintings which was about to be shipped to America. I thought it would be safe there in the art galley. But I was wrong."

On arriving in New York, Liane learned that that particular painting had already been sold to Mr. Twiggin. He phoned the art gallery, inviting her to be guest of honor at his mansion.

"I would have gone," the artist went on,

"but later that same day I was almost run down by a car. And I got a scary phone call, warning me not to accept his invitation."

"What did you do?" Nan asked anxiously.

Her question was answered by Jacques Dupré. He explained that he had fallen in love with Mademoiselle Renard several months ago and had asked her to marry him. "She knew I had once been in prison and understood the ways of criminals," he added, "so she telephoned me in Paris and asked me to fly to New York and help her."

Soon after arriving, the former thief realized he was being shadowed. He cleverly shook off the man who was following him and flew secretly to Elm City.

Dupré went on, "I intended to recover the letter which had been hidden behind Mr. Twiggin's painting. This would help us prove someone was holding Liane's grandfather a prisoner. At the Elm City

Airport, however, I read in the newspaper that the police were expecting me to try and steal the painting. As an ex-thief with a prison record, I knew there was little chance to convince them why I had really come to Elm City."

Bert grinned. "So you pulled your scarecrow trick in order to sneak up to the mansion."

"*Oui*. I realized Liane's unknown enemy was trying to trap me and have me thrown in jail to stop me from helping her. So I knew I would have to operate under-cover."

Bert turned to Liane Renard. "What about that repairman? Did you try to con-tact him?"

"Oh, yes," the artist nodded. "The name he signed was Tim Jensen, and the company he worked for was Videolectric Products. I learned it was located in Elm City, and I called the firm as soon as I got to New York. But they told me he had been fired and had moved to California."

"Probably your enemy got him fired!"

"I am sure of it," Mademoiselle Renard agreed.

Nan looked thoughtful. "What was your mother's family name before she married? Mightn't that help in tracing your grand-father?"

"Perhaps. But I do not know it. My mother resented the way her parents had acted, and would not even talk about them. So I never learned her maiden name. She always signed herself merely as 'Anne C. Renard'—for Anne Carol Re-nard."

Nan was silent a moment, then flashed a sudden startled glance at her brother. "Wait! How did your mother spell her middle name?"

Liane raised her eyebrows. "C-a-r-o-l, I suppose. Is that not how Carol is most often spelled? Of course, I do not actually know, since she never wrote it out. Why do you ask?"

Bert exclaimed, "Because we know someone else with that name—only it's his *last* name!"

"Yes—Hubert G. Caryll," said Nan, "spelled C-a-r-y-l-l, and he's the manager of the Lion Manufacturing Company in Elm City!" She explained how he had come to the Bobbseys' house, trying to get hold of the bronze key.

Liane Renard and Jacques Dupré were surprised and excited by this news. Perhaps her mother's maiden name had been Anne *Caryll*! "If only we knew what that key was for!" Liane fretted.

Bert snapped his fingers. "Maybe there's a way to find out!" He looked for a phone booth in the park and called his father. "Dad, didn't you tell us you attended a dinner in honor of that old locksmith when he retired?"

"You mean Jason Ives? Yes, indeed," Mr. Bobbsey replied.

"Do you know where he went to live?"

"At Pleasant View Condominium, I believe, on Lakeshore Road, right in Elm City."

"Thanks a lot, Dad!" Bert told the others what he had learned. Liane Renard volunteered to drive there in her rented car. The condominium turned out to be a high-rise building in a lovely parkland setting, especially designed for elderly retired persons.

Jason Ives—a lively, ruddy-cheeked man with flowing white hair—seemed happy to receive visitors. He enjoyed talking about his work and recognized the bronze key at once. "I made a set of keys like that years ago for a Mr. Leo Caryll." With a chuckle, the old locksmith added, "I can tell by that curlicue symbol stamped on the key. It stands for Leo the Lion!"

Nan asked, "Then did Mr. Leo Caryll have anything to do with the Lion Manufacturing Company?"

"He certainly did, my dear—he *owned* the company! And those keys were made for a tower he built overlooking the lake. You can see it from my window."

The twins gasped and reached out to squeeze each other's hand. Both were sure they already knew the tower Mr. Ives was talking about!

10

Tower of Secrets

The old locksmith led his visitors to the window. "There it is," he said, pointing to a tall slender building far off on the lakeshore. The tower was outlined vividly in the glowing red sunset. "Looks almost like a lighthouse, doesn't it?"

Bert nodded excitedly. "My sister and I saw it when we were at the beach. It's built on a rocky point that juts out into the lake."

"That's right, my boy. I'm told Mr. Caryll used it as a restful hideaway from his business duties. It's a beautiful place on closer view!"

The Bobbsey twins and their friends thanked Jason Ives and left. All were impatient to visit the tower, which they felt sure held the answer to the mystery they were trying to solve.

Jacques Dupré took the wheel and they started off along Lakeshore Road. At Bert's request, however, they stopped briefly at a drugstore. He came out clutching a flashlight. "Thought we might need this—just in case," he explained.

Jacques Dupré grinned. "*Oui*, good thinking!"

Their destination lay west of Elm City. Dupré turned off the highway onto a blacktop road which led out over the point. Ahead, the tower loomed darkly in the dusk, its windows unlit.

Dupré stopped the car on a paved terrace which bordered the building. All four got out and regarded the tower in keen suspense.

"Looks like no one's home," Bert murmured.

"That need not stop us from looking inside," said the Frenchman. "Did you bring that key?"

Nan handed it to him and they approached the door of the building. Dupré knocked twice. When no one answered he tried the key. It fitted the lock perfectly and the door opened.

Bert switched on the flashlight and shone it from side to side. They were in a white-walled-room which seemed to take up most of the ground floor. It was bare except for a table, some chairs and several white ceiling-support columns.

A small oil painting was leaning against the wall on one side of the room. Liane uttered a glad cry as Bert's flashlight beam illuminated the canvas, revealing a French chateau, a farm field and a scarecrow. "It's my picture! The one that was stolen from Mr. Twiggin!"

Jacques Dupré found a light switch and

they rushed to examine the painting. Liane turned it around and probed gently with her fingers between the wooden frame and the canvas. Presently she pulled out a folded piece of paper.

"Your letter!" Nan exclaimed.

Liane nodded happily. "Yes, and now the police will know I'm not just making up a story about my grandfather—and that Jacques is innocent!

"Whoever phoned Mr. Twiggin," said Bert, "must have stolen the painting just so the crime would be blamed on Monsieur Dupré!"

"And I'll bet that person," Nan said, "is also holding Miss Renard's grandfather a prisoner!"

"Perhaps in this very tower!" Jacques pointed to a door with an arrow-like indicator above it. "That is an elevator, I think. Shall we see what is on the upper floors?"

"You bet!" Bert said adventurously.

The door slid open at the touch of a wall

button. Inside were six more buttons, one for each floor, plus an emergency stop. "Let us begin our search on the top floor and work our way down," Jacques suggested.

He pressed the proper button and the elevator rose smoothly. But halfway up, it stopped!

"What's the matter?" Liane asked.

"I am not sure," the Frenchman replied uneasily. He pressed the button again, then tried all the others, but nothing happened.

Suddenly a sneering laugh rang out. *"No use jabbing those buttons, Dupré. The elevator will remain right where it is, with all of you in it!"*

The twins and their friends looked around in dismay to see where the voice was coming from. "There!" said Jacques Dupré, pointing to an upper corner of the ceiling. "A closed-circuit television camera and loudspeaker!"

"How sharp-eyed of you to notice, Frenchy!" Their unseen enemy chuckled unpleasantly. "Too bad it will do you no good!"

Nan felt sure she had heard the same voice before, but it took a moment to figure out where. "That's Mr. Caryll!" she blurted. "Hubert G. Caryll—the man who came to our house!"

The speaker chuckled again. "Quite right, my dear. I knew you twins and Miss Renard and her thieving boyfriend would find your way to this tower sooner or later. So I set a trap, and you all fell right into it."

"What do you intend to do with us?" Liane exclaimed.

"Nothing! Just leave you stuck there until someone discovers your plight— which I assure you is not likely to happen soon. When the police do arrive, they will assume you let yourselves in with that stolen key and accidentally got trapped.

After all, Jacques Dupré is a known criminal. Until then—*au revoir!*"

Silence followed. As the Bobbseys and their two friends stared at each other, Bert whispered, "Don't worry! When I stopped in that drugstore, I phoned home again to let Mom and Dad know where we were going. They're bound to come looking for us eventually!"

"Good boy!" Jacques patted his shoulder. "Meantime, let us see what can be done to get us out of here." He pointed to an inspection panel in the top of the elevator. "That may provide an opening big enough to squeeze through. I was trained as a circus acrobat, you know."

Leaping up, he knocked the panel cover loose and grabbed the edge of the opening. Then he hoisted himself like a gymnast, working first one arm and then his head and shoulders through the opening until he was able to squirm out onto the roof.

"What are you going to do?" Liane asked.

"Climb the elevator cable, if I can."

Peering up through the opening, the others could see him start to shin his way upward, hand over hand. The cable was greased, which made his task much harder and messier.

Suddenly the three inside the elevator felt a jerk, then a slight sinking feeling.

"We're going down!" cried Bert.

Jacques Dupré dropped back inside to join them as the elevator continued its gentle descent to the ground floor. The door opened and Nan exclaimed, "Daddy!"

Mr. Bobbsey was waiting outside with a police officer. Nan rushed into his arms.

"Oh, boy, are we ever glad to see you!" Bert added. "We were trapped in that elevator!"

"A button was stuck on the second floor," his father explained. "One of the policemen who went up to investigate discovered it. He and another officer are still up there."

"How did you know we were trapped, Daddy?" Nan asked.

"I didn't know, honey. After Bert phoned, I decided it was high time the police were brought in on this case. And from the look of things, it's lucky they were!"

After introducing Liane and Jacques, the twins related what had happened. As they finished telling their story, a police sergeant brought down two handcuffed prisoners—Mr. Hubert Caryll and a sullen-faced woman in a white smock, who turned out to be the housekeeper.

"Old Mr. Leo Caryll's still up on the top floor," the sergeant reported. "He's ill and helpless. Officer Norton's keeping him company for the time being." Pointing to Hubert Caryll, he added, "It seems this guy and his lady stooge have been holding the old man prisoner. They were just going to lug him downstairs when we showed up."

"P-p-please, may I see him?" Liane Renard begged in a trembling voice. "I am sure he is my grandfather!"

A tearful but happy scene took place when the two met for the first time. Later, the Bobbseys and Jacques Dupré looked on as Leo Caryll told his story. Even though the old man was in his eighties, the others could see a strong resemblance between him and Liane.

He explained that after he fell ill and retired, his distant cousin Hubert had taken over control of the Lion Manufacturing Company. Hubert expected to inherit the firm and was furious when he learned the old man was trying to get in touch with his long-lost daughter Anne. To stop him from trying again, Hubert paid the housekeeper to hold the man prisoner in the tower, where a closed-circuit TV camera kept him under constant observation.

One day the TV broke down. The housekeeper gave Mr. Caryll a pill to put him to sleep while a repairman was brought in to fix it. But the old man cleverly avoided swallowing the pill so he could get the repairman to smuggle out a message and mail it to France. Unfortunately, the housekeeper discovered one key was missing and figured out what had happened.

This was what led Hubert Caryll to stop at nothing in his efforts to keep Liane Renard from ever finding her grandfather. As a friend and guest of Mr. Twiggin, it had been easy for him to steal the painting. He confessed to the police that he had smuggled it out of the mansion in his overnight case after the house party, hoping Jacques Dupré would be caught and jailed for the crime.

Next day, the Bobbsey twins were

interviewed on television by the reporter called Vince. "And what can you tell our viewers about this latest mystery you've solved?" he inquired.

For a moment, the young detectives were sad that their adventure had come to an end. But, to their surprise, they would soon be involved in another one called *The Haunted House Mystery.*

Meantime, Freddie answered the TV reporter. "Don't ever be sure scarecrows aren't alive. *Sometimes they can walk!*"